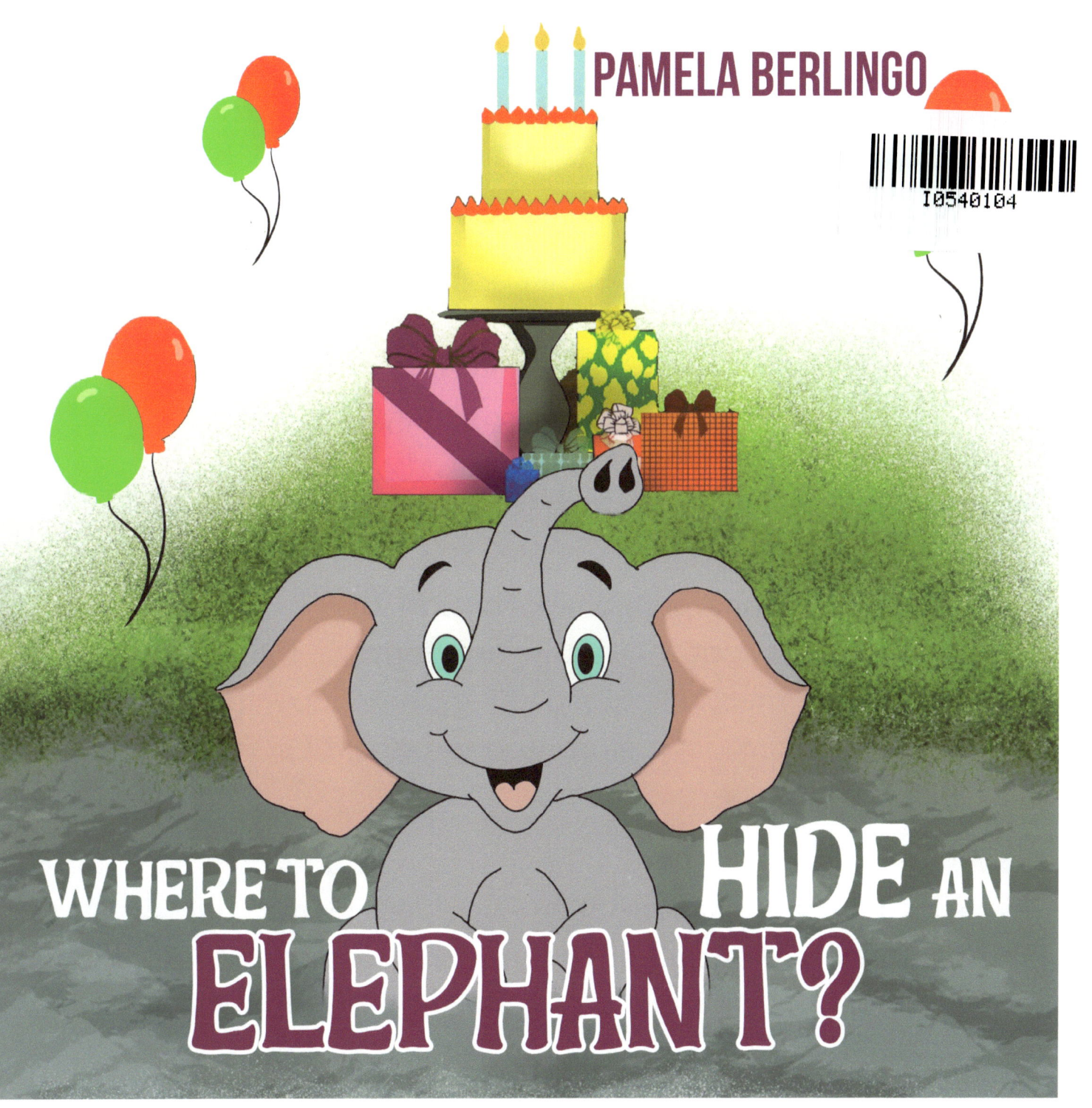

DEDICATION

TO MY FAMILY, WHOSE LOVE AND SUPPORT CONTINUE TO INSPIRE ME EVERY DAY:

TO MY HUSBAND, FOR HIS UNWAVERING BELIEF IN ME,

TO MY PARENTS, FOR THEIR ENDLESS ENCOURAGEMENT AND GUIDANCE,

AND TO MY BELOVED PUPPIES, STELLA AND FINN, AND MY SWEET CAT SAMMY.

FOR FILLING MY LIFE WITH JOY AND COMFORT.

THIS BOOK IS FOR ALL OF YOU, AND FOR THE READERS WHO SHARE IN THE MAGIC OF STORIES.

WITH LOVE AND GRATITUDE.

AND WITH SPECIAL THANKS TO SYDNEY REDMOND FOR HER BRILLIANT IMAGINATION AND TALENT.

PAMELA BERLINGO

TABLE OF CONTENTS

ACKNOWLEDGEMENTS

SYDNEY REDMAN WHO BROUGHT THE BOOK TO LIFE WITH HER BEAUTIFUL AND FUN IMAGES OF GEORGE AND HIS FRIENDS.

INTRODUCTION

Join George, the elephant, at the birthday of his best friend Jenny the giraffe. There is cake and presents and so many fun games to play. Also, so many friends gathered together, celebrating his best friend's birthday! Sounds like fun, right?

But there is one teeny tiny problem; where do you hide an elephant for the hide-and-seek game? Come join the party to find out how and where George finds the perfect hiding spot!

Once again, Pam has created another book that provides a fun and learning gateway for children and parents alike. The story will unravel a heartwarming tale for families and friends, teaching them unconditional friendship and love!

George's eyes opened as soon as his alarm rang. He jumped out of his bed, flapping his big ears in excitement, and sprinted to the door.

Today was the day; his best friend's birthday!

He was so excited!

Let's back up a bit. George is an elephant. He is 7 years old and a bit over-excited to be getting together with his friends. It's been a long summer. He had spent most of the time around the house, only getting to meet some of his friends once or twice a week.

But now, since everyone was going to be at Jenny's party, George was more than ready for a fun afternoon and ready to play with his friends.

"Mom! Mom!" George trumpeted loudly to make sure he was heard.

"Can I go to Jenny's a little bit early today?" He asked as he danced around in a little circle around his mom.

"I promised her that I would help her get the game set up today," he informed his mom, hoping that she would let him go a bit earlier.

"Yes," replied his patient mom.

"You can go a little early. Just don't forget Jenny's gift, and make sure you are polite to everyone," his mom advised with a sigh. She knew there was no stopping her wonderful, son from enjoying his friend's party. His sparkling eyes were full of excitement.

George knew he had to get ready quickly if he were to reach Jenny's earlier than others.

He ran outside in the backyard, where they had a natural pond, and jumped right in. It was a bit cold, but he didn't have time to waste. He sucked in a big trunk full of water and sprayed himself all over!

Next, he rubbed his trunk, head, body, and sides on the nearby tree. He wanted to look especially nice for the party so he could see Jenny and all his friends

"I wonder what everyone did this summer..." murmured George to himself. When he finished getting ready, he went inside and grabbed Jenny's gift. He then said goodbye to his mom and headed out on the path to Jenny's house.

George made his way through the trees and looked around. The sun shone through thick layers of leaves, creating a beautiful canopy. "Wow, today is sunny and nice," thought George.

"What a great day for a birthday," he added as he walked further, wagging his small tail.

Jenny who is his very best friend, was amazing. She was smart and had so many friends. She always knew just what to say to everyone and made friends easily. He couldn't wait to wish her a "Happy Birthday" and help her set up the place for the party.

As he rounded a familiar corner, he saw Jenny and her family. "Hi, Jenny! Happy Birthday" George shouted excitedly.

Jenny, the giraffe, was busy hanging some streamers. As soon as she heard George's voice, she turned her long neck around to see him and smiled, "Hi George, it's so good to see you!"

Jenny walked elegantly toward George with her long legs. She bent down and nudged him with her nose.

"I am so glad you are here," she said, her beautiful brown eyes filled with awe and happiness. "We are going to have so much fun seeing everyone today, aren't we?" Jenny asked George, gesturing over all the decorations and food.

"We are going to have a blast," said George, in total agreement with Jenny.

"Oh, here is your present. Where should I put it?" George said, holding out the gift he had brought.

"You can put it over on the table by the tree. It is just beside the table where the cake is," said Jenny. "Mom said that's a safe area," Jenny added, rolling her eyes.

"I think she thinks we will run and break everything, so she put the food and the presents over there," Jenny laughed, and George joined in.

"Jenny, the cake is HUGE!" George said, looking at the cake sitting high on the table. "I can't wait to have some; it looks just yummy!" he added, pretending to lick his lips for the added effect. He just loved anything sweet, especially cakes!

"Me too," said Jenny.

"Mom has been keeping it away from all of us since morning!" she said, pouting, expressing her disappointment.

Just as they were talking, Jenny's mom suggested they pick out some games and get them ready before everyone else arrived.

Jenny and George agreed and walked over to a shaded green tree-filled area to make their plans.

"We can play tag," suggested George.

"Definitely!" Jenny agreed wholeheartedly. It was one of her favorite games. The tag was always fun, and they could run all through the trees and not bother anyone!

"How about Hide-and-Seek?" Chipped in Jenny.

"Sure, that sounds fun," said George. "Then it's off to the cake so we can eat!" Laughed George!

"Agreed. Sounds fun!" said Jenny, letting out a stream of giggles.

Well, that settled it. The games had been planned, and the fun was just about to begin.

It was time to welcome more guests and friends!

Right after they planned the activities, the guests started arriving.

The first one to arrive was Luke, the Tiger. He was the most popular student in the jungle school. He was fast and strong and usually won all the games they played. Luke was already running toward them with his big paws getting ahead of him.

He slid in next to Jenny and said, "Happy Birthday, Jenny! You're going to have a great party today". He wagged his tail and sat down.

"Thank you, Luke! I am glad you came," Jenny replied with a smile.

He then looked at George and greeted him, "Hi there, George! How has your summer been?"

Both Jenny and George filled in Luke on their summer break and asked about his as well.

It was such a good time to be together again!

As the three were talking, two more friends arrived; Ben, the beetle, and Julie, the alligator. The first one to say hello was Julie. She was getting so long now. Her thick skin and deep black eyes shown with excitement to see her friends again. "Happy Birthday Jenny," said Julie and added, "Hi to everyone!" to greet the rest.

Jenny and everyone all jumbled together their hellos and updated each other on their summers.

As everyone chattered and talked about their holidays, there came a small voice from below, "Happy Birthday, Jenny!"

It was Ben, the dung beetle. Sometimes, they all forgot he was there. He was so small and quiet. But once they noticed him, they all shouted a "hello" back, and Jenny bent way down and gave him a soft nuzzle to say hello.

Next to arrive was Eddy. Eddy was a parrot. His feathers were green and white, and yellow. He was the class clown, always swooping in and doing something to stir up some mischief.

"Happy Birthday Jenny!" Sang out Eddy with a swoosh and landed on the tree next to where everyone was gathered.

"Let's get this party started," he laughed in delight and spread out his wings wide.

With all of her friends now at the party, Jenny offered everyone food. They ate together while chatting and had fun catching up.

Luke suggested, "let's play some games, everyone."

"I feel the need to win today!" he added with a laugh.

They all laughed at what Luke said and joined in on the idea. They spent time playing tag and running around. Luke, as self-predicted, was the winner of most of the races.

"Let's play hide-and-seek," said Jenny.

"Luke," said Jenny, grabbing his attention, "since you won most of the games, tag, your it!"

They all laughed, and Luke went to a tree, facing the trunk, closed his eyes, and began counting. He counted to 100, so the others could hide. All of George's friends started to hide. It was only then that George realized he didn't know where to hide as he was huge! An elephant!

Where on earth do you hide an elephant?!

He ran to Jenny, his best friend, and asked, "Where should I hide?" He seemed worried because everyone had already found a spot to hide.

Jenny, with her height and long legs and neck, also had a similar problem. But she said she was hiding among the tree trunks as she could hide behind those.

She offered George to join her there, and he thanked her for that. But he knew he would just give her hiding spot away. He knew that he couldn't hide behind those trees. He was much too wide for that spot.

He then asked Ben where he was hiding, and he said behind the small rock by the tree. George knew he couldn't hide behind a small rock either; he was far tall for that.

Next, he asked Eddy to suggest where he should hide. Eddy told him to go up high.

"No one ever finds me there," Eddy added.

"I am heading to the top of that tree over there," Eddy pointed to where he was heading with his bright green wings.

George knew that climbing up there was out of options, too, as an elephant can't climb a tree or fly.

What now? Where should or could he hide?

George then went to Julie.

"Julie, I need some help. Where can I hide? I am out of all ideas, and there doesn't seem to be anywhere for me to hide. I am an elephant; I am too big and can't fly. Where should I go?" Julie thought and thought.

She finally said, "George, I am heading to the long grass area over there so I can blend in and stay low, but that will not help you."

George's face fell in disappointment, but Julie quickly added, "But as I was searching for my spot, I thought of a great place for you to hide."

George was excited now. "Really, Julie? Where is that?" He asked, his eyes hopeful.

With that, Julie whispered in his ear, telling him where he should hide, and so he did.

Luke continued to count loudly so everyone could hear the approaching deadline to find a hiding spot.

He eventually finished counting, "96, 97, 98, 99 and 100......Here I come!" He announced.

Luke then rushed around and found Jenny hiding behind the tree trunks, then Ben behind his rock. He then climbed up the tree to find Eddy. Luke looked and looked, then found Julie hiding in the tall grass.

But where was George?

He was confused. He looked in the trees high and low. He looked behind rocks and even under a few just to be sure.

NOTHING.

He then looked in the grass again but still couldn't find George. He went all the way down by the water. Again, there was no George.

Finally, he gave up and called out, "Come out, come out where ever you are, George."

Everyone waited and waited.

Where was the Elephant??

Finally, Julie started to laugh, and George poked his head out from behind the…..

Oh….! So that's where he had been hiding all the time!

The birthday cake!

George hid behind the birthday cake!

That's where you hide an elephant!!!

Everyone laughed, and George was declared the winner
of hide-and-seek.

The game was over, and they all gathered together
around the cake.

Everyone shouted, "Happy Birthday, Jenny," as she cut
the cake and then they all had cake!!!

The end.

About the Author

PAMELA BERLINGO GREW UP IN THE PICTURESQUE TOWN OF TUNKHANNOCK, NESTLED IN THE HEART OF NORTHEASTERN PENNSYLVANIA. SURROUNDED BY THE BEAUTY OF THE ROLLING HILLS AND SMALL-TOWN CHARM, PAMELA DEVELOPED A DEEP LOVE FOR STORYTELLING THAT HAS STAYED WITH HER THROUGHOUT HER LIFE. SHE NOW RESIDES IN PENN TOWNSHIP, HANOVER, PENNSYLVANIA, WHERE SHE LIVES WITH HER SUPPORTIVE HUSBAND, HER PARENTS, AND A LIVELY HOUSEHOLD OF PETS -TWO PLAYFUL PUPPIES, STELLA AND FINN, AND A WISE CAT NAMED SAMMY.

WHILE PAMELA'S PROFESSIONAL LIFE INCLUDES SUCCESSFUL CAREERS AS A REAL ESTATE AGENT AND INSURANCE AGENT, AS WELL AS SERVING AS A COMMISSIONER FOR PENN TOWNSHIP. PAM WAS HONORED TO BE A GRADUATE OF THE "ANNE B. ANSTINE EXCELLENCE IN PUBLIC SERVICE SERIES" HELPED TO GUIDE HER IN WORKING IN THE COMMUNITY. THE AUTHOR'S PASSION HAS ALWAYS BEEN WRITING. HER FIRST BOOK, MAX'S TRIP TO THE ZOO, WAS A HEARTFELT DEBUT, AND SHE CONTINUES TO POUR HER LOVE FOR THE WORLD AROUND HER INTO HER STORIES. PAMELA FINDS INSPIRATION IN HER MEMORIES, HER EXPERIENCES, AND THE PEOPLE SHE ENCOUNTERS, WEAVING THESE ELEMENTS INTO VIBRANT TALES THAT RESONATE WITH READERS OF ALL AGES.

WHEN SHE'S NOT WRITING, PAMELA ENJOYS SPENDING TIME WITH HER FAMILY AND PETS, EXPLORING NEW PLACES, AND SAVORING THE SIMPLE JOYS OF LIFE IN HER HOMETOWN. THROUGH HER WRITING, SHE HOPES TO SHARE THE MAGIC OF CHILDHOOD WONDER AND THE POWER OF IMAGINATION WITH READERS EVERYWHERE.

THE END

SPECIAL THANK YOU AND CREDIT FOR SYDNEY REDMOND FOR HER AMAZING CHARACTERS AND IMAGINATION.